Star Sisters
and the
Royal Wedding

Written by Jennifer Blecher

Illustrated by Anne Zimanski

Disclaimer: This is a work of fiction. Some characters within it are based on living persons. However, all actions, statements, and thoughts attributed to such characters, and all other events and incidents depicted in this work, are either the products of the author's imagination or are used in a fictitious manner.

TO JEFF.
FOR READING EVERY PAGE, EVERY TIME.

Chapter One

At the end of the street was a forest. A hidden forest. Or maybe it wasn't really hidden so much as no one ever went there, which is surprising given how beautiful the forest was, with a fresh water stream that ran underneath a creaky wooden bridge and a large clearing where wildflowers grew high and thick. But the kids in town were busy, with soccer practice and ballet classes and birthday parties on the weekends. Everyone rushed to and fro, coming or going, going or coming. Sometimes it seemed like the only kids in the entire town who weren't busy were Coco and Lucy, two girls who didn't even know each other.

You see, Coco and Lucy were new to the town. They weren't signed up for soccer or ballet and they didn't know anyone who was having a birthday party. Coco had just moved to the town from Paris where the people said *"Bonjour,"* not "Hi," and ate croissants for breakfast, not bagels. Coco's mother said, "Coco, either help me unpack or go outside and play."

Lucy had just moved to the town from the city, where she lived in a small apartment with an elevator that rattled and groaned and clanked when it moved. Up, up, up... Lucy would ride until she reached her home high above the treetops. Lucy's mother said, "Lucy, you have a backyard now. Go outside and get some fresh air."

So each girl left her new home in search of something to do. Of course, both Coco and Lucy were hoping to find something really fun and exciting, like an abandoned box full of brand new puppies or a secret rose garden with a fountain of singing birds at the center. But honestly, they would have settled for anything, anything at all. So Coco wandered down the street and Lucy wandered down the street. And that is how they found the forest. Or maybe the forest found them. Either way it was surely fate, maybe even destiny, which led Coco and Lucy to the forest. It was one of those days at the end of spring when the warm winds of a storm were just starting to blow. *Whoosh,* the wind seemed to say as it rustled the leaves on the trees. *Get ready, for soon I will grow stronger and rattle the sky.*

But at that moment the sky was still blue and the sun was still shining. Lucy entered the forest first, following a worn dirt path through the large evergreen trees until she saw the stream and wooden bridge. She walked to the middle of the bridge, kicked off her flip-flops, and dipped her toes in the cool water. It wasn't a box of puppies, but at least the water felt good on her feet.

A few minutes later, Coco entered the forest. She followed a different dirt path that ran between two boulders and past the field of wildflowers. But pretty soon, she also found the stream. Seeing Lucy, a girl who looked about her own age sitting on the wooden bridge all alone, Coco decided to walk over and say hello. But as soon as she set foot on the bridge it shifted and *moan, crack, crash!* the wooden bridge collapsed and both Lucy and Coco fell right into the stream.

Don't worry, they weren't hurt. This was a gentle stream, not a rushing one, so the girls were safe and sound (although their bottoms did get quite wet). What matters most, you'll soon realize, more than wet underwear or even the tiny minnow fish that swam by and tickled Lucy's leg, is that Coco and Lucy were brought together. By magic? By fate? By pure luck? We'll never quite know for sure. But what we do know is that their meeting was one thousand years in the making. And that's a very long time.

One thousand years ago there were no phones with games, cars with televisions, or sneakers with Velcro. There weren't even phones, or cars, or sneakers at all. But there was jewelry. Women of noble birth wore beautiful necklaces made of jewels that were unearthed from deep in the ground. Craftsmen spent months melting down gold and silver to weave the intricate patterns that formed the chains and settings for the jewels.

Not much has survived from one thousand years ago, but two very important necklaces have. And both those necklaces happened to be hanging around the necks of Coco and Lucy, two regular girls plopped together at the bottom of a stream.

Chapter Two

Lucy pushed her long brown hair out of her eyes. Mud was splattered on her cheeks and the tip of her nose. She looked at Coco, the blond-haired girl sitting next to her in the stream, and asked, "Who are you?"

"I'm Coco," said Coco. "Sorry about breaking the bridge. Bet you weren't expecting a swim today."

Lucy laughed and stood up, straightening her wet shorts. "Here, let me help you," she said.

No sooner had Lucy reached out to take Coco's hand than a mysterious, miraculous, marvelous thing happened. The birds stopped chirping, the chipmunks stopped scampering, and the  trees of the forest seemed to lean into one another like athletes in a huddle, blocking out the sun and turning the fore

"What's going on?" asked Lucy.

"I don't know," said Coco, looking around. "Just hold on tight to my hand, we'll be okay."

The girls helped each other climb out of the stream, grabbing on to exposed roots and large rocks. They wanted to leave the forest, but the trees had moved in such a way that they weren't sure which direction was out. So they made their way to an overturned tree trunk that was covered in thick green moss and sat down, still clutching each other's hands.

Boy oh boy, Coco and Lucy were scared.
But thankfully not for long. Because before
they could even think of what to do, or
where to go, the tree trunk they were sitting
on started to move. It felt like popcorn was
heating up underneath the moss, a gentle
rumble that grew and grew until – *POP!* A
tiny old woman with flowing gray hair and a
long silk dress appeared before them. She
was the size of a doll and glowed gently,
lighting up the dark forest like a fancy crystal
chandelier.

"I knew it!" said the little woman as she
danced in tiny silly circles, her arms and legs
flailing about. "I just knew it! I knew this

day would come! I had my doubts, of course. One thousand years is a long time to wait, in a tree trunk nonetheless. But I didn't lose faith. I never gave up. No, I did not! And now here you are. Here *they* are."

The little woman stopped dancing and stared at the necklaces around Coco's and Lucy's necks. She put her hand to her mouth and sighed. "Oh, what a long, long

time it's been since I've seen those royal jewels."

Coco and Lucy looked down. Somehow, in all the commotion, both girls had failed to notice that they were wearing matching necklaces. The necklaces each had a large stone carved in the shape of a star hanging on a thick silver chain. But neither girl would describe the dangling star as a jewel, no way. The stars were beautifully shaped, but they were also dull and dirty, not at all sparkling or colorful. Still, there was no denying that the necklaces were special; unlike any necklace you'd ever see in a store.

Yet there were Coco and Lucy, staring at an identical necklace on someone else's neck.

"Don't worry my dears," said little woman. "I'll explain everything in due time. But first, tell me about those necklaces you're wearing."

"I found mine on a sidewalk in Paris," said Coco. "I was walking home from school, throwing rocks into the river like I did every day, when I noticed something peeking out from a gutter. When I looked closer I saw this necklace. I was worried someone was looking for it so I posted a sign saying, "Necklace Found. Call Coco.""

necklace found

call coco

My mom wrote our phone number on the bottom. But when no one called, my mom said I could keep the necklace. I know it's old and dirty, but for some reason I just love it. Maybe it's the shape. Isn't the star so neat?"

Lucy nodded. "Super duper neat," she said. "I found mine in my grandma's attic. I was searching through a leather trunk full of her old ball gowns when all the dust made me sneeze. *Ahh-choo!* Next thing I knew this necklace was there, resting right on top of the dresses. My grandma said she'd never seen it before and she let me keep it. Although she said she couldn't imagine anyone wanting such a dirty old thing. I guess it is old, and it *was* really dirty, but I loved the necklace from the moment I saw it. I haven't taken it off since."

"Very interesting, my dears," said the little woman. "But here's the first thing you need to know: YOU didn't find those necklaces. The necklaces found YOU."

Chapter Three

"Get comfortable, girls," said the little woman. "I've clearly got some explaining to do." She leapt onto a nearby stone and cleared her throat. Coco and Lucy wiggled their bottoms into the cool soft moss of the tree trunk. Their legs kept tapping into each other, which made them laugh. They felt a little nervous, but a good kind of nervous. You know, the feeling that tingles deep inside your belly when you're not really sure what is about to happen next, like on the first day of school or when you close your eyes right before a surprise.

"First, let me start with a proper introduction," said the little woman. "I'm Grissella Arista Encanta Ignanacia. And you are?"

"Lucy," said Lucy.

"Coco," said Coco.

Grissella sighed. "Well, in that case, just call me Grissella," she said. "Hmmm... Where to start? Where to start?" She tapped her wrinkled cheek with one of her tiny fingers. "The beginning? No, not the beginning. The end? No, no, not quite right either. Let's see... I've got it! I'll start in the middle. For the middle is always a good place to start."

Coco and Lucy smiled. Grissella was a silly little creature, the way she darted about with her long gray hair and formal dress. She reminded the girls of a grandmother fairy – a very energetic and kooky grandmother fairy.

"Now," continued Grissella, "the middle is a good place to start because all was well in the middle. In the middle, the land was thriving, peaceful, and happy. You see, my dears, I come from the land of Illustria. A land of natural beauty and riches, and also a land of magic. There was a river in Illustria that was fast and strong and deep, with water so clean and crisp that people traveled from all across the land just to take a sip. Travelers brought drops of water back to their sick relatives and those relatives got better. Pregnant women drank from it and gave birth to strong, beautiful babies. Eventually we began to understand why there was no sickness or strife in Illustria: we had been drinking water touched with magic."

Magic. It was such a great word. Full of wonder, possibility and...

"And that's when everything turned bad," continued Grissella, jarring Coco and Lucy from their thoughts. "The King and Queen of Illustria were kind. They spread the word far and wide that everyone should bring their sick, their weak, and their needy to come drink from our magical river. And they came.

Before long,
Illustria was the
most powerful
kingdom in the
land, full of

farmers, teachers, scientists, and artists."

"What's so bad about that?" asked Lucy.

"Nothing," said Grissella. "If it hadn't been for the evil Queen Callista. Queen Callista ruled the kingdom next to Illustria. She wanted the river's water all for herself. So she spent years and years digging a trench, trying to divert the river's path to her own kingdom. But no matter how deep she dug, the river stayed its course, straight through Illustria. Queen Callista, however, would not give up. She decided that if the river would not come to her, she would go to the river. She trained an army of scoundrels, men with hearts so dry and shriveled that they did whatever Queen Callista ordered, no questions asked.

Queen Callista and her army invaded Illustria, banishing our King and Queen to a land so far away that they were never heard from again."

Chapter Four

"That's horrible," said Coco.

"How sad," said Lucy.

Grissella nodded and wiped a tear from her tiny eye. "But the story doesn't end there," she said. "The King and Queen of

Illustria had two daughters named
Esmeralda and Mathilde. They were
mischievous little princesses, always telling
jokes when they should have been quiet,
skipping when they should have been sitting
and, most troublesome of all, disappearing."

"You mean like playing hide and seek?"
asked Coco. "I love a good game of hide
and seek."

"I bet there are all kinds of great places
to hide in a palace," said Lucy. "Hidden
staircases, enormous cauldrons, chests full of
jewels."

"That's all true," said Grissella. "But
when I said disappearing, I meant the

abracadabra kind of disappearing. The
princesses would simply vanish!"

"No way," said Coco, her eyes wide.

"Cool," said Lucy. "How'd they do that?"

"I'm not quite sure," said Grissella. "But
I know it had something to do with their
necklaces. You see, one day a scientist
found two emeralds along the shore of the
river. He brought the emeralds to the King
who had Illustria's master jeweler carve each
emerald into the
shape of a star
and place it on a
necklace. The
King gave these

necklaces to his daughters with the words: 'May the magic of our mighty river seep into these emerald stars and inspire you to spread kindness throughout the land.' A short time later, I started noticing that the princesses would simply disappear – *poof!* – returning after a bit with smiles on their faces. I don't know where they went or what they did, but I knew they were happy and together."

"Maybe they traveled through time," said Coco.

"Across the ocean to far away places," said Lucy. "Like the jungles of Africa to cuddle with baby lions."

"Or the North Pole to swim with the polar bears," said Coco.

"Well, I guess anything's possible," said Grissella. "All I know for sure is that on the day of the invasion I was bathing the princesses in the river when I saw Queen Callista's army approach. I turned to

Esmeralda and Mathilde and said, 'Quick, girls. Use your magic. Disappear!' Next thing I knew they took each other's hands, said some words, and were gone."

"What happened next?" asked Coco. "To the princess sisters?"

"I don't know," said Grissella, shaking her head. "I've wondered that same thing every day for a thousand years. I hope they were safe and loved and happy. I hope they grew to be old ladies with gray hair and families of their own. And seeing those necklaces around your neck, I think I finally know a little more."

Coco and Lucy each touched her necklace. "Our necklaces?" asked Lucy.

Grissella nodded. "They weren't always yours. Those necklaces used to belong to the princess sisters of Illustria."

"No way," said Coco.

"Yes," said Grissella. "Yes, indeed."

"But our necklaces aren't made of emerald," said Lucy. "They're just stones. Stones in the shape of stars. Maybe they just *look* like the princesses' necklaces."

Grissella shook her head. "I am absolutely certain that those are the same necklaces. I would recognize the shape of the star anywhere, with its delicate points.

And notice how the chain is braided in such a complicated pattern? That is the work of Illustria's master jeweler. Sure they're a little dull and dirty, but remember, those necklaces are one thousand years old."

"But how did the necklaces end up here, with us?" asked Coco.

Grissella climbed down from the stone she had been standing on and sat next to Coco and Lucy on the tree trunk. She shrugged. "I don't know. That's why I started my story in the middle, not the end. The next thing I remember about that horrible day, after I sent the princesses away, was taking a deep breath and diving into the river. The river must have saved me with its magic. It must have shrunk me and washed me into a tree trunk to wait."

"Wait for what?" asked Lucy.

"I'm not entirely sure," answered Grissella. "But I'm starting to think I was supposed to wait for the necklaces to be brought together again – to wait for two girls with the same spirit as the princesses to find them. I think I was supposed to wait for the two of you."

Chapter Five

Grissella yawned and rubbed her eyes. After spending one thousand years in a tree trunk she was exhausted from so much talking. She needed to sleep. So Coco and Lucy said their good-byes, promising to come back soon. As they walked away, the evergreen trees loosened their huddle, the animals resumed their daily noisy work, and the sun's rays once again shone down on the forest at the end of the street. It was almost as if nothing happened, except that so much *had* happened.

Coco and Lucy skipped out of the forest two very different girls from the ones who had stumbled in just a short time before. Both girls had entered the forest alone and unsure of themselves, unsure of their new surroundings and what they would do on that lonely day while everyone else was busy. But they exited together, with the sense that their lives were about to change forever. They had been chosen. For what, they weren't exactly sure. But they couldn't wait to find out.

In the meantime, Coco and Lucy had some important things to discuss. Things such as tiny Grissella and how she had been trapped in a tree trunk for one thousand years. How their necklaces had once belonged to princess sisters in an ancient magical land. How the necklaces found them, not the other way around. But for each girl there was one other important thing that she was thinking but didn't quite know how to say.

Eventually, after covering important topics like their favorite colors (Coco's was bright pink, but also sometimes yellow, and Lucy's was teal, but also sometimes purple), Lucy stopped walking and said: "You know, there's something else I should probably tell you."

"What?" asked Coco.

"Well, it's kind of silly," said Lucy as she kicked at a pebble on the ground. "But you should probably know that I've never had a best friend."

"Never ever?" asked Coco. "Not even for one day at recess?"

Lucy shook her head. "Never ever at all."

"Me neither," said Coco. "At least, I don't think I have. I never really knew how you got one."

Coco and Lucy walked a little further, the sun shining on their backs, until they came to a large crack in the sidewalk. It was wide and wiggly, the kind of mean looking crack that you simply could not walk over without a plan.

Coco stopped. "You know," she said. "We could be best friends. You and me."

"That's a great idea," said Lucy. "But how do we do it?"

"I don't really know," said Coco, shrugging her shoulders. "How about we jump over this crack as a test. If we land on the other side at exactly the same time, it will mean we were meant to be best friends."

"Good idea," said Lucy. "On the count of three. One, two, three. *Go!*"

Coco and Lucy bent their knees and sprung into the air, their hair flying and their arms raised high. When they landed on the other side of the crack at exactly the same moment, it felt as if they had jumped into a completely new world.

"We did it!" said Coco. "It worked!"

"That was amazing!" said Lucy. "What do we do next?"

"We should probably start with a name," said Coco. "Something that we call ourselves."

"How about Star Sisters," said Lucy. "Because of our star-shaped necklaces."

Coco smiled. "That's perfect," she said. "The Star Sisters."

"Friends forever," said Lucy.

"Through thick and thin," said Coco.

"We're both in!" said Lucy.

"Lucy, look," said Coco. "The star. On your necklace. It's glowing! The stone is turning green. Like an emerald!"

"Yours is, too," said Lucy. "It's beautiful."

"Grissella was right," said Coco. "These must be the princesses' necklaces. And there must still be some magic left in them. Come on, let's go back and show Grissella what happened."

Coco and Lucy turned back towards the forest. But as soon as they joined hands, a crazy thing happened. The light from their emeralds combined and glowing stars began to circle all around them, like a crown of bright sparkling light. When the light faded a few seconds later, they were nowhere near the forest. Not even close.

Chapter Six

The next thing they knew, Coco and
Lucy were standing on a raised platform in
front of a large mirror. The room looked
like a dressing room in a store, only much
bigger and more grand, with a carved ceiling
and lights dripping with crystals.

"What just happened?" asked Coco.
"Where are we?"

"I have no idea," said Lucy. "But I know
where we're not, and that's home."

Suddenly Coco gasped, her eyes wide.
"Lucy," she said. "Your necklace. The star
is still glowing. Like an emerald. It's so
bright."

"So is yours," said Lucy. "Amazing."

"Do you think this is what Grissella was talking about?" asked Coco. "With the princess sisters? How they used to vanish?"

"Maybe," said Lucy. "This definitely feels like an abracadabra kind of thing."

Before they had time to say anything else, the door to the dressing room opened.

"Oh, thank goodness," said a woman with a British accent who was carrying a wicker sewing basket. "The flower girls are finally here. Welcome to London. I'm Mary, the royal dressmaker. We are dreadfully behind schedule, just dreadfully. My seamstresses have been working day and night to finish the lace for Princess Caroline's dress. They're exhausted and now I have to fit both of you all by myself. Come on now and stand up straight. I need to get your measurements."

"Flower girls?" said Coco.

"Princess Caroline?" said Lucy.

"Oh, dear me!" said Mary. "I know we're not supposed to call her Princess Caroline just yet. At least not until after the wedding tomorrow. After all, she doesn't have one drop of royal blood, not that such a thing matters to the likes of me. That girl's got more poise and grace than a whole gaggle of royal children all wrapped together and tied in a bow. But please don't tell the Queen.

She's such a stickler for titles."

"The Queen?" asked Coco.

"Yes, the Queen," said Mary. "Caroline is marrying the Queen's grandson, Prince Wellington. And you two are going to be the flower girls in their wedding. But you already know all that, so please cooperate. Now raise your arms and hold still."

Coco and Lucy looked around. Through a doorway they could see a large room filled with sewing machines, silk fabric, and piles and piles of lace. At the center of the room was the most beautiful wedding dress Coco and Lucy had ever seen. It had long lace sleeves and a wide skirt that was sewn with so many flowers, patterns, and pearls that it looked as if the skirt could tell an entire story.

"Takes your breath away, doesn't it?" asked Mary when she noticed Coco and Lucy looking at the wedding dress. "A true work of art. Now just make sure you don't tell anyone a word about it. Not a peep.

We've kept the dress secret for months. Not a single detail leaked, not a one. The whole world's been waiting to see this dress and tomorrow they'll all see it together for the first time when Caroline walks down the aisle at Eastminster Abbey."

"The whole world?" asked Coco with a gasp.

"Oh yes," said Mary. "You do know they're calling this the royal wedding of the century, don't you?"

"What does that mean?" asked Lucy.

"It means you girls had better stay still and let me pin these dresses because there are going to be a whole lot of people watching you tomorrow," said Mary. "Now, about these beautiful necklaces. I assume you'll want to wear them at the wedding?"

Coco and Lucy looked down at their necklaces. The emeralds were glowing strong and bright. The girls weren't quite sure what was going on but they were certain that their necklaces had a lot to do with it.

"Yes!" they said at the exact same time.

Chapter Seven

After Mary finished fitting their flower girl dresses – sewing pearl buttons here and silk sashes there, adding a poof to the sleeves and some trim to the hem – Coco and Lucy were escorted into a black cab that whirled them through the city of London. They passed elaborate churches with goblins

carved in stone, a tall clock tower that
chimed on the hour, and a Ferris Wheel so
enormous that it took riders high up into
the clouds. But nothing compared to where
they ended up.

"Here we are,"
said the driver of the
cab. "Luckingham
Palace. Home of the
royal family. You
young ladies here for
the royal wedding tomorrow?"

"Yes," said Coco. "At least, we think so."

"I knew you two were royalty with
necklaces like those," said the driver.

Before Coco and Lucy could respond, a tall guard wearing a black feathered hat and a red jacket with gold buttons down the front opened the cab door. He didn't say a word, but he motioned with his hand for Coco and Lucy to follow.

And follow they did, right through heavy double doors to the glistening, glimmering, gold covered entrance hall of Luckingham Palace. The walls were covered in mirrors and crystal chandeliers hung from the ceiling causing flecks of light to dance all around the room like leaping ballerinas. The black-and-white checkered floor would have been perfect for hopscotch and, under

normal circumstances, Coco and Lucy

would have jumped right on. But these

were not normal circumstances.

"This is definitely not the forest,"

whispered Coco.

"Not at all," whispered Lucy back.

Suddenly, a kind voice floated down the

hall. "Oh, lovely," said the voice. "You

must be Coco and Lucy. Prince Wells said

you would make the most wonderful flower girls and I can see immediately that he was right. I'm Caroline."

"Princess Caroline?" asked Lucy, even though with just one look she knew that this woman had to be Caroline. She was very pretty, with a big smile and long brown hair. But more than that she was just... hmmm, what was it about her? Well, she was just matched. Her shoes matched her dress, which matched her jacket, which matched the tiny hat that perched on her head. Lucy herself favored a little more spunk when it came to dressing, but she admired Caroline's style nonetheless.

"Oh please, just call me Caroline," said Caroline with a smile. "After all, I'm not really a princess until tomorrow, right?" She took each girl by the hand. "Come on," she said. "I'll show you to your bedroom."

"Here?" asked Coco. "In the palace?"

"Of course," said Caroline. "After all, you're family."

"I guess," said Lucy with a shrug.

Chapter Eight

"This is really weird," said Lucy as soon as Caroline shut the bedroom door behind them.

"Eyes popping out of my head weird," agreed Coco.

"Eyes popping out of my head and then rolling down a hill and falling into a lake of slimy goo weird," said Lucy.

"Exactly," said Coco.

The girls plopped down on the enormous bed. The comforter was so fluffy it seemed to exhale underneath them. It was the first time that Coco and Lucy had been alone since this magical journey began. Lying there in the center of the huge bed, in a

room in Luckingham Palace, which is in London, which is the capital city of the

United Kingdom, which is located on the continent of Europe, which is all just a long way of saying that Coco and Lucy were very far from home, and they couldn't quite believe what was happening.

"The last thing I remember was deciding to call ourselves the Star Sisters," said Lucy.

"Me, too," said Coco. "I remember saying:

'Star Sisters, friends forever.
Through thick and thin, we're both in.'

Then we held hands and the next thing I knew we were surrounded by light and we ended up here."

"And the stones on our necklaces turned into glowing emeralds," said Coco.

"Yep," said Lucy. "And now everyone thinks we're the flower girls for the wedding of Caroline and Prince Wellington."

"Caroline even thinks we're related to Prince Wellington!" exclaimed Coco.

"They think we're *royalty*," said Lucy with a twinkle in her eye. This turn of events was pretty confusing, but she had to admit, it was also pretty cool. She could certainly stand being treated like royalty for a while.

"Like the princess sisters of Illustria," said Coco. "Maybe we're here because of them. After all, Grissella did say that the necklaces found us, not the other way around. She said the necklaces were waiting for two girls with the same spirit as the princess sisters. Two girls who could carry on their work of spreading kindness."

"Which means we're not just here to enjoy the royal wedding," said Lucy.

"Don't think so," said Coco.

"But then what exactly *are* we here for?" asked Lucy.

"Beats me," said Coco. They rested their heads on their hands, but before they had time to think of what to do next, Coco and Lucy heard the sound of crying coming from down the hallway.

"I think that may be a clue," said Lucy. "Come on. Let's investigate."

Coco and Lucy crept down the carpeted hallway trying not to attract attention, which is not an easy thing to do in a palace, especially when everyone thinks you're part of the royal family. Maids carrying piles of

freshly folded towels stopped and curtsied. Butlers carrying trays of food with silver lids bowed their heads. "Your highnesses," they said softly, which made Coco and Lucy giggle. Eventually, the girls made it to the room where the crying sound was coming from. Coco and Lucy put their heads against the door and listened.

"Caroline, you can't be serious!" said an angry voice coming from inside the room.

"Please, Poppy, it wasn't my decision," said Caroline's voice. "I didn't have a choice. Maybe when I'm actually a princess, but until then..."

"Until then, you're still you," interrupted Poppy. "You're still my sister. Or has that changed just like everything else?"

"Poppy!" said Caroline. "How could you say that? I love you."

"Then act like it," said Poppy. "Act like the sister I know."

"I am the sister you know," said Caroline. "I'm trying my best."

"You know what, just leave," said Poppy. "I want to be alone."

Coco and Lucy stepped aside just in time to see Caroline rush out of the room in tears. She ran down the long hall and disappeared.

A few seconds later, Poppy came to the
door and noticed Coco and Lucy. "Oh,"
she said, surprised. "I didn't think anyone
was here. I'm Poppy, Caroline's sister. You
must be Coco and Lucy. You might as well
know what's going on. After all, we're all in
this wedding together."

Chapter Nine

Coco and Lucy followed Poppy into her room. Hanging on the front of a large wooden chest was an ivory colored silk dress with puffy short sleeves and a calf-length skirt. A silk sash was tied around the waist.

It looked identical to the dresses that Coco and Lucy had tried on earlier that day, only in adult size.

"I guess we'll all be twins tomorrow," said Poppy. "Only you two will look adorable and I'll look like an adult dressed up as a flower girl."

"Are you a flower girl, too?" asked Lucy. Poppy was clearly too old to be a flower girl, but who knew how these royal weddings worked. It had been a strange day from the get go.

"My point exactly," said Poppy with a sigh. "I'm the maid of honor. But the Queen told Caroline that all the dresses should match so this is what I'm supposed to wear. No offense to you guys, but I'm way too old to wear a dress like this."

Now, Coco and Lucy didn't know much about high fashion, but they did know what it felt like to not want to wear something. Like Coco's jeans with the scratchy seam that rubbed the inside of her leg, or the cardigan sweater that itched her neck when it was buttoned the wrong way. And then there were Lucy's tights that bunched up in her shoes. Those tights were terrible!

"And the worst part is that Caroline knows how much I hate this dress," continued Poppy. "But she won't stick up for me. She's too worried about upsetting the Queen. Caroline thinks that since we're not of royal birth she has to be extra careful about how she acts and what she says. Not that you guys would understand, being royalty and all."

Coco and Lucy wanted to correct Poppy, to tell her that they weren't of royal birth either. They weren't Prince Wellington's cousins! They weren't royalty! They weren't even British! But Poppy had turned away, lost in her own thoughts.

"You know, it's not even about the dress," she finally said. "If Caroline liked the dress I would wear it just to make her happy. The problem is that I feel like I'm losing the sister I know and love. The one who was fearless and always by my side, who would stand up for me against anyone. I feel like I'm losing my best friend."

It was sad to see Poppy upset, the way her long brown hair fell in front of her face as the sun began to set over the city of London. But at least Coco and Lucy knew what they had been sent to do: help Poppy and Caroline fix their relationship before it was too late. The problem was, now that they knew what their challenge was, they had no idea how to solve it.

Chapter Ten

The girls left Poppy in her room and
started back down the long hallway. "We
have to find Caroline," said Coco. "She's
the only one who can help Poppy feel
better."

"And we have to act fast," said Lucy. "The wedding is tomorrow morning. We don't have much time."

"But where do you think Caroline is?" asked Coco.

"I have no idea," said Lucy with a shrug. "This palace is enormous."

The girls looked around. The hallways seemed to stretch on forever; everything was one big blur of closed doors, royal portraits, and candelabras.  "Let's just start walking," suggested Coco.

So walk they did. Down hallways, up winding staircases, through glass doors, and underneath crystal chandeliers. Finally, after several twists and turns, they saw something they recognized: the black-and-white checkered floor of the entry hall.

"Game of hopscotch?" asked Lucy.

"I thought you'd never ask," said Coco with a giggle.

Hip, hop, crisscross, skip, jump, land. Coco and Lucy were having so much fun that they forgot where they were and what they were supposed to be doing. But then they heard the sound of high heels approaching and it all came flooding back. The girls froze.

"Oh, please," said Caroline kindly. "Don't stop playing for me. You girls look like you were having so much fun. The kind of fun I used to have. Rather, the kind of fun *we* used to have." Caroline's voice trailed off and she walked over to a large window.

"You mean you and Poppy?" asked Lucy.

"Yes," said Caroline. "We grew up in an old stone house surrounded by rolling green hills and fields of buttercup flowers. We'd spend hours playing hopscotch in the courtyard. One time Poppy even caught a

frog and trained him to jump with us. We named him Harold. But that was before. Before all of this."

Caroline motioned out the window at the busy London street. People were piled up outside the palace's iron gates pointing and taking pictures. Red double-decker buses slowed their speed as the passengers strained to get a peek.

"See all those people outside," continued Caroline. "The ones who are trying so hard to see inside this palace? They think life is perfect in here. That it's all royal balls and tea parties and sparkling tiaras. But it's not like that at all. Palace life comes with rules and obligations. Don't get me wrong, I'm excited to become a princess, but there are things I will miss. Things like..." Caroline stopped talking and looked down at her hands.

"Things like Poppy?" asked Coco in a quiet voice.

"Yes," whispered Caroline. "I miss my best friend."

"Well, then," said Lucy. "Let's get her back."

"How?" asked Caroline. "Poppy thinks I've changed. That I'm not the same sister

I've always been. How can I convince her that's not true?"

Coco and Lucy looked at each other. It was one thing to want to  solve a problem, but quite another to know how to do it. But this was their first mission as Star Sisters and they were determined to figure it out. Luckily, they didn't have to figure it out alone, for just at that moment Mary the seamstress walked up.

"Oh, thank heavens!" said Mary. "Just the girls I was looking for. I always get so lost in this big palace, don't you know. I have your dresses for tomorrow. All pressed and ready for the big day and... Oh my!" Mary gave a startled jump when she noticed Caroline by the window. "Your highness. I didn't see you there. My apologies." Mary bowed deeply.

"Not to worry," said Caroline. "I was just thinking."

"About what, your highness?" asked Mary.

"Oh...well...um," stuttered Caroline.

"She was thinking about Poppy," said Coco. "You see, Caroline and Poppy are trying to figure some things out."

"What kind of things?" asked Mary.

"Well," said Caroline. "We're having a bit of a disagreement over Poppy's dress for the wedding tomorrow. I know the Queen wants Poppy's dress to match the flower girl dresses, but Poppy really doesn't like the way it looks. She wants to wear something more grown-up. Something that reflects her personality, her style."

"Well, of course she does!" said Mary. "Coco and Lucy are girls, Poppy's a woman. Their dresses should look different."

"But what about the Queen?" asked Caroline.

"What about *you*?" said Lucy. "What about *Poppy*?"

Caroline took a deep breath. "You know what," she said. "You're right. This whole time I've been worrying about the Queen, about what she thinks and about what she wants. I've lost sight of what I think, of what I want. And worst of all, I've lost sight of the most important person in my life, my sister. My best friend."

Mary smiled. "Well, I think I know a way we can fix this little problem."

"You do?" said Caroline.

"I do, indeed," said Mary with a sharp nod of her head. "But I'm going to need some help. First, show me to Poppy's room and then I'll explain my plan."

Coco, Lucy, and Mary followed Caroline as she led them to Poppy's room. Luckily, Poppy was out and the room was empty. They grabbed Poppy's dress from its hanger and snuck the dress down the hall to Coco and Lucy's room.

"We're going to sew Poppy a brand new dress," explained Mary once she closed the door behind them. Mary pulled out some thread, a few pins, a pair of scissors, and three sewing needles from her bag.

"This is going to be a little tricky," she continued. "I don't have enough time to go back to my sewing room and there's not much fabric here to work with. But I think if I cut this seam here, and sew a new neckline there, with a low drape in the back, I just might be able to make this work. Yes, I think I can make this work quite well."

And work they did. For hours Mary put Coco, Lucy, and Caroline to work. They held pins, threaded needles, and cut fabric.

When Mary winked at Caroline and said: "Not exactly how a princess usually spends the night before her wedding, is it?" Caroline just laughed.

"There's no where else I'd rather be," she said with a big smile.

It was true, Caroline looked happier than Coco and Lucy had ever seen her. And in the end they made a dress that they knew Poppy would love. With barely any time to spare, they snuck back into Poppy's room and placed the new dress on its hanger.

Chapter Eleven

The next morning was bright and sunny. Everyone in the wedding party met in the throne room of Luckingham Palace to take official photographs. Coco and Lucy arrived early, nervously awaiting the moment when Poppy appeared in her brand new dress.

"Look, there she is," said Coco as Poppy

entered the room. "She looks so happy."

Poppy sure did. The new dress was

lovely, modern and simple, befitting a royal

maid of honor. It was maybe a tad bit short

on fabric, a little on the skimpy side, but Poppy's smile made up for any shortcomings. When Caroline saw her sister, her smile was just as wide.

"So," said Caroline. "What do you think of your new dress?"

"It's perfect," said Poppy. "I feel like... I feel like me!"

"You look like you," said Caroline. "Like the sister I know and love."

"So you're okay with this?" asked Poppy, spinning in her brand new dress. "You're not worried about what the Queen thinks?"

"Not anymore," said Caroline. "I've been doing a lot of thinking. Not about the Queen, or the wedding, or even Wells. I was thinking about you, my sister. Family is what matters most, not what other people

think or what they say. I'm going to be a modern princess, which means I speak my mind and fight for what I believe in. And I believe in you, Poppy. I should have stuck up for you. Because that's what sisters do. We stick together through thick and thin."

"Hey," whispered Coco. "That's our line."

Lucy laughed. "We'll let them borrow it just this once."

Click, click, click went the photographer's camera, capturing all the pre-ceremony joy and happiness. Suddenly, it was time for the wedding. Just as Mary predicted, Princess Caroline stunned the world in her gorgeous lace wedding dress. As she stepped out of the car with her father, you could almost hear the entire city of London gasp.

But they weren't just gasping at Caroline.
Poppy was standing right behind her,
straightening Caroline's train and
supporting her with the kind of love only a
true friend can provide. The next morning,
a picture of Caroline and Poppy ran on the
front page of the newspaper. "*Royal Sisters
Steal the Show*," said the headline.

Coco and Lucy had a pretty grand time as
well. At the wedding ceremony they walked
down the long red aisle of Eastminster
Abbey, each holding one of Poppy's hands,
taking in all the fancy guests in their crazy
hats and topcoats. Then they returned to
the palace for the wedding reception. But as

the emerald stars on their necklaces started to fade, they knew it was time to go back home.

But how? Well, that's a good question. They figured they'd leave the same exact way they came. As the party continued, with the champagne flowing and the canapés passing, Coco and Lucy took one last look at Luckingham Palace.

"Not too shabby," said Coco.

"Nope," agreed Lucy. "But it's not home."

So Coco and Lucy held hands and said the magic words that brought them to London in the first place:

"We're Star Sisters, friends forever.

Through thick and thin, we're both in."

And sure enough, a flash of light and a blink later, Coco and Lucy were back where they started, on the sidewalk by the forest at the end of street. But here's the thing — even though it was the same sidewalk, by the same forest, in the same town — everything felt different. Coco and Lucy had each other now. Like Caroline and Poppy. They were Star Sisters. They didn't know what the future would hold, but they had a funny

feeling there were going to be many more adventures to come.

"Come on," said Coco. "Let's go tell Grissella what happened."

"But wait," said Lucy. "What *did* happen exactly?"

Coco laughed. "I'm not entirely sure!" she said.

"Oh girls, I'm so proud!" said Grissella after Coco and Lucy explained their adventure. "The roaring river of Illustria may have shrunk to this tiny stream, but the spirit of our kingdom lives on."

"What do you mean?" asked Coco.

"You spread some kindness today," said Grissella. "You helped two sisters who were upset get back together. That is what Illustria was all about, spreading kindness and helping people."

"Plus, attending the royal wedding of the century was pretty cool," said Lucy.

"Super duper cool," said Coco.

"Now, go on you two," said Grissella. "Take those necklaces of yours and wait. I have a feeling you'll be called to help again soon."

Coco and Lucy waved good-bye to Grissella and made their way back home. The stars on their necklaces were back to stone, but they didn't mind. They knew the stars would be glowing emeralds again in no time.

THE END

Can't get enough of the Star Sisters? You're in luck. Coco and Lucy are just getting started. Here's what's next...

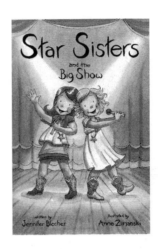

Trina Fast loves to be up on stage with the microphone turned up high and her guitar in her hands. But when Trina writes a song about her friend Lake for the summer camp talent show that hurts Lake's feelings, she learns an important lesson about the power of her own voice.

It's summertime and Coco and Lucy are ready to dive into the swimming pool and another great adventure about the meaning of friendship.

Figure skaters Nina Kerrington and Tara Harling have dreamed of going to the Olympics since they laced up their first pair of ice skates. But when Nina falls and hurts her knee the day before the qualifying competition, it turns out that her slip was more than just an accident.

Get ready as Coco and Lucy take to the ice to help a little girl learn a whole lot about sportsmanship, kindness, and the importance of saying "I'm sorry".

www.star-sisters.com

K.J. Dowling has big dreams of writing a
book. But when no one takes her seriously, K.J.
starts to doubt herself. It's Coco and Lucy to the
rescue in an urban adventure in the city where
dreams come true – NYC.

Join the girls as they make their way through the
Metropolitan Museum of Art, around Central
Park, and down 5th Avenue to show one special
little girl that being different is a good thing and
believing in yourself is even better. An inspiring
read for everyone with big dreams.

www.star-sisters.com

Visit **www.star-sisters.com** for star necklaces,
coloring pages, book bundles, and all
the latest information on where
Coco and Lucy are popping up next.

Westgate Publishing
WP

28109870R00067